my LiTTLE PONY

Creative Colouring Book

ORCHARD

yum

ORCHARD BOOKS

First published in Great Britain in 2016 by The Watts Publishing Group

7 9 10 8 6

HASBRO and its logo, MY LITTLE PONY and all related characters are trademarks of Hasbro and are used with permission.

A CIP catalogue record for this book is available from the British Library.

ISBN 978 1 40834 293 0

Printed and bound in China

MIX
Paper from
responsible sources
FSC
www.fsc.org   FSC® C104740

Orchard Books

An imprint of Hachette Children's Group

Part of The Watts Publishing Group Limited

Carmelite House

50 Victoria Embankment

London EC4Y 0DZ

An Hachette UK Company

www.hachette.co.uk

www.hachettechildrens.co.uk

This book
belongs to

Imogen Johnsn

Aeg: 6

Come and explore the
magical kingdom of Equestria.

Inside this book you'll find hundreds of intricate illustrations and
pretty patterns, all waiting for you to bring them to life.

You can use pens, pencils or crayons to colour in each page. But why
stop there? Add extra details, patterns and pictures, too - let your
imagination run wild! The most important thing is to relax, get
creative and have lots of fun.

Look out for your favourite My Little Pony pals as you turn the pages.
How many friends can you spot?

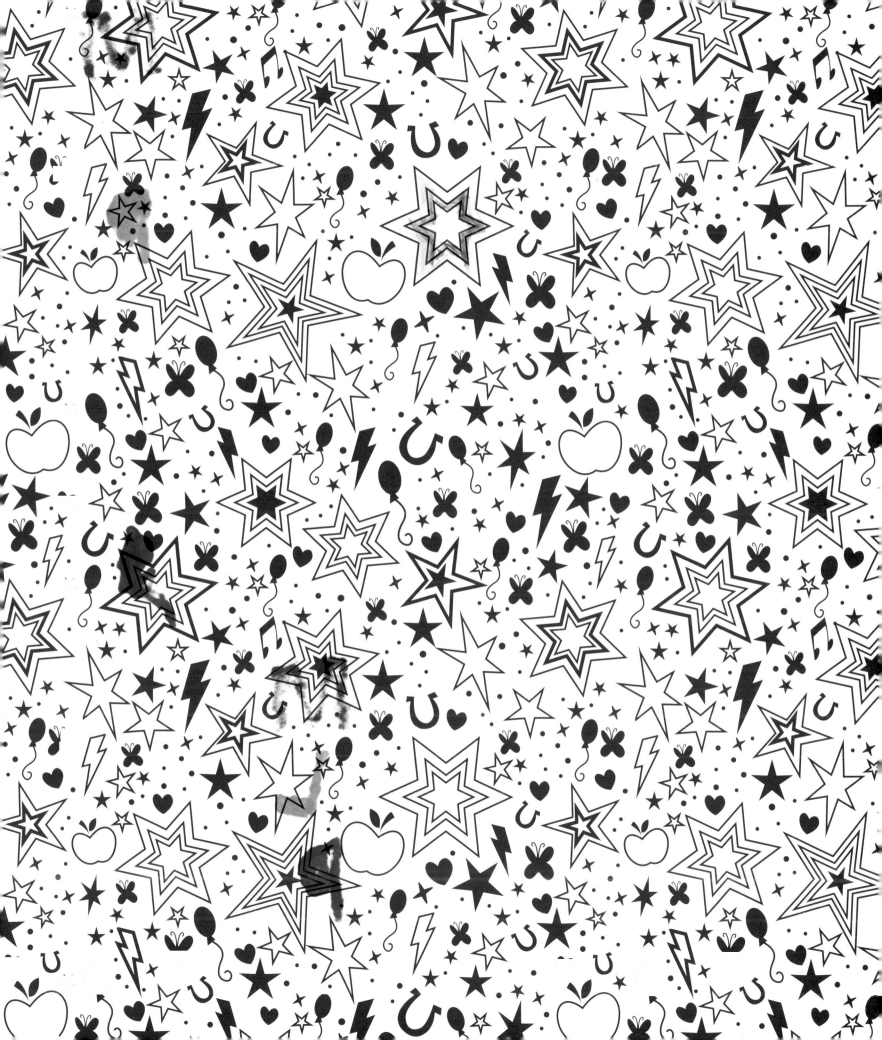